Shadowy Technicians

Shadowy Technicians. Copyright © 2000 for the Authors

Acknowledgements on page 149 constitute a continuation of this copyright notice.

No part of this publication may be reproduced, stored in a retrieval system or transmitted, in any form or by any means, without the prior written permission of the publisher or, in the case of photocopying or other reprographic copying, a licence from the Canadian Copyright Licencing Agency (CAN©OPY), 1900-1 Yonge St, Toronto ON M5E 1E5. Ph 416 868-1620, 1-800-893-5777, fax 416 868-1621, admin@cancopy.com www.cancopy.com

Design and in-house editing by Joe Blades.
Cover: *365 small paintings of chandeliers*, oil on board, various sizes, (installation detail) by Andrea Mortson copyright © 1997-99
Printed and bound in Canada by Sentinel Printing, Yarmouth NS

The Publisher gratefully acknowledges the support of the Canada Council for the Arts and New Brunswick's Arts Development Branch.

 cauldron books is a series edited by Ottawa writer/editor/publisher rob mclennan. It is named after the Celtic idea of the cauldron as the keeper & dispenser of wisdom & knowledge. The series will focus not only on worthwhile collections of poetry, but on single author collections of essays, as writing on writing. cauldron books are published by Broken Jaw Press. rob may be reached at <az421@freenet.carleton.ca>

 **Broken Jaw Press**
Box 596 Stn A
Fredericton NB E3B 5A6
Canada

www.brokenjaw.com
tel / fax 506 454-5127
jblades@nbnet.nb.ca

Canadian Cataloguing in Publication Data
Main entry under title:

Shadowy technicians

(Cauldron books : 1

ISBN 1-921411-71-5

1. Canadian poetry (English) — Ontario — Ottawa.* 2. Canadian poetry (English) — 20th century.* I. McLennan, Rob, 1970- II. Series.

PS8295.7.O8S53 2000   C811'.5408'0971384   C00-950030-8
PR9198.3.O8S53 2000

Shadowy Technicians

New Ottawa Poets

rob mclennan, editor

cauldron books 1

Fredericton • Canada

Shadowy Technicians
New Ottawa Poets

Introduction, by rob mclennan	9
Stephanie Bolster	13
Lamp	14
The Skin Beneath Fingertips	15
Eggs	16
Onomatopoeia	17
Jealousy	18
To Speak of Authenticity	19
Cow Meets Moon	20
Two Ways of Regarding Radishes	21
Index Finger	22
Portrait of Alice as Dodgson's Universe	23
In which Alice visits Pacific Rim National Park	24
In New York, Before Moving from Vancouver	25
Moving, Again	26
Richard Carter	27
Canada	28
Lake Mazinaw	29
Thirst	29
Mr. and Mrs. Blackburn Hamlet	30
Things	32
Founder	33
Voice	34
Accountant	35
Laurie Fuhr	37
shallow	38
Mind's Exercise	39
Witness	41
It Must be the End of the World, Because ...	42
The Shaky Hand	43
the merqueen's parlour	45
Old Man Moriarty	46

Wired In 47
Pride 48
accident 49

Robin Hannah 53
  Indulgence, or Off with her Head! 54
  Crossbow on Argyle 55
  December 25 '91 — The Big Panic 56
  The River Groove 57
  Pubic awareness activities 59
  A fair bit and well worth it 60
  her relations with scent 61
  peace tower scaffolded 62
  Love in a cemetery 63
  being at cottage 64
  Oh to whistle 65
  zen 66

Jim Larwill 67
  FLIPPING DOUBLE HELIX COIN 68
  Post-Modern Ljóσaháttur 69
  Trauma 70
  KISS 71
  REFLECTION 72
  Broken Heart 73
  NEUTRAL GROUND 74
  THIS SPRING I HEARD THE HARMONIOUS
    CLAPPING OF HANDS 75
  Trilobite Laughter 77
  I WHISPER LOVE 79

Clare Latremouille 83
  schedule 84
  cave drawing 85
  of eternity 87
  theories on the human animal 89
  in which we discuss the passage rites of manhood 90
  d. June 17, 1989 91
  d. December 13, 1977 92

NEW OTTAWA POETS

    riding hood   93
    Yalecom Valley   94
    slumber party   95
    moving boxes   96
    try sleeping   97
    Garden I-V   98
    Gardening Tips   100

Karen Massey   101
    In the Pub Named for the Irish Expat Writer We Idolized in School   102
    In the Kitchen With Some of Matisse's Women   104
    For the Stones in her Pockets   106
    Slyvia Plath in Heaven Does Tie Dye   107
    Whining Is No Longer Fashionable   109
    Bullet   110
    Patients' Lounge: Day Surgery   112
    Post Biopsy: Recovery Room   114
    Forbidden Words   115

rob mclennan   117
    featherlite   118
    sky, like a thesis   119
    people & skyscrapers & waves   120
    my brother, ludwig   121
    paraphrasing don mckay   122
    train   123
    ferry delay, terminal   124
    death & death & other poems about origin   125
    blowing a new day into a new season   126
    the other eye the final hieroglyph   127
    winter when our minds fill up with snow   128
    and how we slowly began to look like her   129
    japan in my own language   130
    waiting for a rescue hours overdue   131

Ian Whistle   133
    remember by   134
    light   135

Virginia slims	136
Virginia maple	137
there was no blood	138
the seventh seal	139
a bout de souffle (breathless)	140
2 poems for Elvis	141
sh(e)	142
four breakfast poems	143
dis-	145
take	146
Acknowledgements	149
About the Cover and Artist	151

NEW OTTAWA POETS

introduction

> It is not illegal to be unhappy.
> A shadowy technician says alternately,
> Breathe, and, You may stop now.
> It is not illlegal to be unhappy.
> — John Newlove, "It's Winter in Ottawa"
> *The Tasmanian Devil and other poems*
> (above/ground press)

Every ten years or so, someone in Ottawa feels the need to produce a variation on a similar theme — a collection of Ottawa-specific poets, whether Colin Morton's *Capital Poets* (1988, Oroborus), *Open Set: A TREE Anthology* (1990, Agawa Press) or *Six Ottawa Poets* (1990, Mosaic), back to the two-volume *Poets of the Capital*, co-edited by Frank Tierney (1972 & 1977). The purpose of *Shadowy Technicians: New Ottawa Poets* is less an attempt at a representaion of the city's poets as a whole than my selection of some of the newer writers that are currently living & working in the city.

Ottawa has always been called a city of poets, & its activity deceptively large for the size & make-up of its mostly-government drone population. (A few years ago, Ottawa had over a dozen self-produced literary journals.) As far as literature goes, ten years is a long time, constituting a generation in itself. The level of activity rises & falls, old faces disappear, & new ones take their place.

When I first started going to open stage readings such as The TREE Reading Series, Orion & Sasquatch, nearly ten years ago, the poets who had emerged in the 80's were slowly pulling back from the open stage, such as John Barton, michael dennis, Stephen Brockwell & Nadine McInnis — still producing more & more significant work but less publically active — as younger writers David Collins, Rob Manery & Karen Massey started making their own noises, learning the stretch of their individual voices.

The literary history of Ottawa has always seemd disjointed, since the century or so since Archibald Lampman published his first poetry collection here, with Elizabeth Smart & Norman Levine out of Sandy Hill between the wars, to Bill Hawkins' Olson experiments (a member of the band The Children, with Bruce Cockburn), Richard Taylor,

SHADOWY TECHNICIANS

Robert Hogg & Carol Shields weaving their way through the late sixties to the late seventies, about the time that Christopher Levenson, *et al*, at Carleton University started a new magazine called *ARC*.

The eighties saw the emergence of, among other things, the First Draft performance group (Colin Morton, Susan McMaster, etc.), making their experiments with sight, sound & draft beer; the maturity of John Barton; Patrick White & Rob MacLeod working on *Anthos* magazine & Anthos poetry books; George Young organizing events like a madman; Dennis Tourbin putting his poems to paint, & michael dennis following the working class traditions of Al Purdy & Charles Bukowski, just as a group of Carleton University students saw the launch of their first issue of *The Carleton Literary* (then, *Arts*) *Review*.

It's a strange city this. No creative writing department at either university around which to gather, only brief courses that profs continually have to defend; no media acknowledgement for any activity unless it's an obit., & events that can have anywhere from seven to seventy people in attendance, but leaning more prominently toward the former. But still the work goes on.

Shadowy Technicians showcases the work of nine poets who have been producing work over the last few years, getting attention both in & outside the city, in a range of styles. Governor General's Award winner Stephanie Bolster's carefully crafted & almost painterly portraits, to Clare Latremouille's poems of deceptive edge & energy, love & its inevitable hurt; Laurie Fuhr's youthful & explosive bursts, tempered beautifully by a deft & subtle hand, against Ian Whistle's staccato gestures; Karen Massey's pointed storytelling, "drowning off-stage like Ophelia", & tales of getting lost, to Robin Hannah's carved & contained poems, filled with passionate chaos; Jim Larwill's journey through a physical & emotional landscape, the work of his hands, to Richard Carter's quiet structure & questions through the art; & finally, my own, rife with bad jokes, & abstract narrative lyrics, where the questions are sometimes more important than the answers.

The collection, admittedly, feels less than complete without also reading the recent first poetry collections by Craig Poile, David O'Meara & Michelle Desberats, all published by Carleton University Press' Harbinger series, who decided individually, for their own reasons, not to be included. As well, there is the work of others, such as Jenny Haysom & Una McDonnell, all names to watch out for.

NEW OTTAWA POETS

    This book, then, is dedicated to those who keep the city's literature moving — John Metcalf, jwcurry & jennifer books, b stephen harding at *graffito*, Brent Robillard & *The Backwater Review*, Seymour Mayne at the University of Ottawa, John Buschek, Rita Donovan & John Barton at *ARC* magazine, Neil, Sean & Kira at The Ottawa International Writers' Festival, The TREE Reading Series, & Randall Ware at the National Library, among many others. For Diana Brebner, sweet & honest suporter of literature, who helped get the process of the book started, & Joe Blades who let it continue.
    & for John Newlove, who continues to set the standard.

rob mclennan
ottawa, ontario
march 2000

Stephanie Bolster

photo © 1999 Patrick Leroux

Stephanie Bolster's first book, *White Stone: The Alice Poems* (Signal Editions/Véhicule Press) won the Governor General's Award and the Gerald Lampert Award. Her second collection, *Two Bowls of Milk*, appeared in Spring 1999 with McClelland & Stewart. She has also won the Bronwen Wallace Award for Poetry (1996), *The Malahat Review*'s Long Poem Prize (1997), and the (m)Öthêr Tøñgué Press' chapbook competition with *Inside a Tent of Skin* (1998). Bolster's poems have been published in literary journals and anthologies internationally. Born in Vancouver and raised in Burnaby, B.C., she moved in 1996 to Ottawa, where she teaches creative writing and works as a writer/editor for the National Gallery of Canada.

Lamp

That one of green stained-glass
from Québec is a marvel
but lights little other than itself.
At least the reading light
casts some glow around.

Of course a lamplit room
is more conducive to procreation
than one illumined overhead.
Whence did our grandparents come?

Just sitting there,
it might be a bulbous sculpture
with someone's hat left on it.
Bigger than a vase, smaller
than a bookcase. When I told you

it was not yet dark enough, where
was my other hand?
Why else their curves?
Their magnificent shadows.

The Skin Beneath Fingernails

If the whorl of the fingertip
marks us as we are, consider

what this other part must mean.
The ocean's floor. We pretend

seashell pink and chipped red, hope
the chosen colour stays. We kiss the small

nails of babies and wonder at life
with little protection. The best

fortune tellers press the nail deep
against the finger and read in the lapse

of colour the curve of our first
love's lip and the new names

we will give our children
when they forget us.

Eggs

I do not mean broken, the yellow iris
staring from the pan, or creamed with butter
and sugar in the big green bowl.

What resonates comes before – the smooth white
arch, the asymmetry, rows balanced in cartons.
An absence of angles, all curves, shells
more delicate than fingernails.

This is potential, the uncracked white enclosing
the idea of a world; gelatinous ocean,
secret sun. Inside my body

a galaxy, stars living out their half-lives. Discrete,
numbered, they nudge each other toward genesis.

Onomatopoeia

Violinback sheen, he said, and I felt
that maple swelling in my hands.

Blackberry scratches me, and *susurration*
winds around my legs some days.

I've never dared to look it up.
Once a poem in my ear caught my breath

and kept it, though I would have turned
away from the mouse-scrawl

of its letters. That one low
stroke of the cello, who knows what notes,

the cellist a heavy-lidded boy who speaks
another, guttural tongue, and everything I want

rises in me for an instant
and is gone – the vanished splash resounds.

Jealousy

is the sharpest eye. Lemons love it.
It's nettles in the wedding

bouquet, the foot that punts
the dead gull. Jealousy snickers

at what the books told you
and is furious at noon

for being brighter.
Cat hiss only aggravates it.

Its feet are blistered
and its long-fingered hands

are meant for old pianos.
They bang out *Chopsticks*.

To Speak of Authenticity

> *Horse and Train*, 1954, Alex Colville. Glazed tempera.

is not to speak at all, to allow the bold horse
to coldly meet the white eye of its fate, the train's rush
blood-warm in its ears. The rails hold
wheel, hold hoof, as the iron sky
holds in the simmering. Nothing is wrong here,

this sky familiar as the inside of the eyelid,
the horse's call inevitable as the train's.
No step stumbled, no texture neglected – each blade of grass
held in the weight of its own shadow
beside the line, beneath clots of steam.
The dark U on the horse's hoof, meant for luck.

All that's withheld is the transport, collision
of two engines. But no slip of the brush
can stop it. It is all there
in the silent huff of breath.

Cow Meets Moon

Moon and Cow, 1963, Alex Colville. Oil and synthetic resin.

She wears the clouds on her body,
rounded like the sky's arc over earth, rounded
like the hills.

The white of her
blued with moonlight,
her black patches so fluid and luminous

she is that sky, reversed.

The moon is made of milk tonight.
Lucent in its tin pail of sky,

it reflects her shape, lazy and rooted
as the ramshackle fence beside her.

It waits for her fulfilment, for the feel of her
udder brushing its upper crescent as she leaps

over, lowing.

Two Ways of Regarding Radishes

> *Untitled*, 1927 and *White Radish*, 1931, Edward Weston.
> Gelatin silver prints.

I. Female

Yes, radish is a woman reclined, indentation
for her parts of reproduction
and for her navel an empty place
the grubs got to. These mimicries designed
to show us how the woman's leg must bend
and why we find beautiful her knees
traced with a soil which cannot be abraded.

II. Flame

Rippled forms like gritted sand left after tide
but arched upwards as fire goes: even hotter
than sand on bare skin or radish
on the tongue, this first lick of forest fire
at the white-barked birches, flicker of the sacred
candle or the human: hands pressed
in prayer. All flesh with a fire in it.

Index Finger

> *Soeur Saint-Alphonse*, 1841, Antoine Plamondon. Oil on canvas.

What her index finger, bound between pages
of a red book, relinquishes: tracing

a lover's nipples, pendant cross. One winter
she wound thick boiled syrup around that

digit and licked until she tasted fingerprints.
Soon, men held her hand too long at parties.

Against father's wishes she shed dresses
for a black habit; taught her finger

to trace this prophecy of ink even in sleep.
Does she, gazing as a sparrow thrusts live

worms into the wide beaks of her young,
use that fingertip to pick free of her teeth

a thread of venison some moose's death
enabled her to eat? Whose sacrifice tastes

stronger? Severed, her finger would seep
a heresy of red across those pages

her finger lies between: pretending it,
like any flesh, does not exist; pretending it is

holy. Soothing an infant's scarlet
gums it would be less worthy.

Portrait of Alice as Dodgson's Universe

He takes her for the youngest star,
whose light hasn't reached him

yet. He anticipates its hour of arrival.
Then suddenly she is already

everything. Once so small through his lens
inside the garden, she's expanding,

her voice echoing untrimmed in hedges,
fingers multiple as cosmos petals

spreading into constellations
that fill his open-shuttered nights.

He asks God to make him good.
The sky does not respond.

Whichever star she was at first
lost amidst a million others sullied

by a haze of smoke and white-hot
thought. Once he shone as clearly as she

once did. Now it's dark, his field
of view obscured by earthly want.

In Which Alice Visits Pacific Rim National Park

You cannot read it, this garden
untended. No flowers, only huge ferns
and driftwood, only ocean. Too much
sand and too few people, a place

far older than the oldest Oxford
stone. The rocks, furred with
greenish stuff, make you slip, soil
your pinafore. The water does not

smell right, no stories drift upon it.
Breakfast makes you cry, marmalade
too runny, dark bread instead
of scones. You want to write

a letter home but words are soggy
like the sugar in your tea. You cannot
speak, just flutter hands like stupid
wings. Only on the road do you feel

a bit at home, its twisting like that
river. Carriages without horses
pass, gone before you can glimpse
their Sunday finery and parasols.

Did you fall from the rowboat, drown
in a mess of green? Did he leave you
flailing as your sisters tried to help,
as his story flowed on? Even here

his words crest white on the waves,
take flight. Their circling is like that
of inland birds returning to where home
used to be, and finding only water.

In New York, Before Moving from Vancouver

> *The Temple of Dendur*, c. 15 B.C., Roman Emperor Augustus.
> Aeolian sandstone.
>
> Originally erected on the banks of the Nile in Nubia, this Egyptian monument would have been submerged as a result of the construction of the Aswan High Dam, begun in 1960. Instead, it was given by the Egyptian government to the United States. Brought to the Metropolitan Museum of Art as a collection of numbered stones, it was reassembled in 1978.

They've laid these stones just so
in replication of their placement before
breaks were made. Hordes of children
in uniforms cavort, threatening gold twisted
ropes and guards put there to keep them
out. Glass walls wedge into the green

of Central Park where homeless faces peer
at history without its dust. Despite photographs
showing stone blocks on barges, I feel like I'm
in Disneyland, where on a replica of a fake
mountain with my family, I stole a pinch of real
styrofoam rock and took it home. Left

alone, the temple might have sat for millennia, sunk
but intact, carved portal guards admitting
schools of fish, each stone correct against the next
instead of slightly off, the hieroglyphics skewed
upon the walls. Which of us is farther from home,
me or stone? Soon, my parents will be waiting

at the airport in the rain of that new city
I have always known. No longer real, the life
I've preserved there. My cells reconfigured;
those who I came from will not know me now.
I know: to save what I love, I will break it
and go, my boxes full of heavy, genuine stone.

Moving, Again

The neighbour's shaved his dog, a shaggy pup
when we moved in, and grown a belly and a bearded
muscled friend with whom he brunches daily
on the balcony, beneath the *fleur-de-lys* umbrella. The dog
licks the friend's ankles. It can see now, a winter of knots
and shit clipped free, it can see what's happening.
The men wear tans under their shorts and look at each other
sidelong. Look at us in here shoving our boxes

to the bright side of the living room, furniture
to the dim. It would be so easy to take everything
from us right now. They might do it, too,
both curious and maybe unemployed, our boxes nestled
up against the window with its blinds stripped. "FRAGILE!"
we've scrawled across each box, clear in either official
language, and so, when we go out for supper, the men
steal them with care to the flabby man's balcony.

We return to find them out there waltzing to my Jacques Brel
in your old blue underwear, their bare chests pressed together for
the first time in surprise, the dog panting.
Gone our two lifetimes of books and all those clothes
I never wear. We lie down on the hardwood floor, dusty
where the bed was, and plan our new apartment,
furnished only with the three-legged table they didn't want,
on which your grandmother gave birth to her first child.

NEW OTTAWA POETS

Richard Carter

Richard Carter was born in Nottingham, England, in 1970, and grew up in Ottawa. He has published one small collection — *Now, then* (England: 1996, Cloud) — and had poems printed in local magazines such as *Hostbox*, *The Backwater Review* and *Bywords*. In 1997, he won Carleton University's George Johnston Award for poetry.

Canada

A land no government can offer. A buried
blank beneath the shovel blade. Light rain
charges pebbles, foams into creeks granite
boulders dying slowly. The sun looks down

on geologic shudder, time that blows
in breeze like spruce, crawls through crevice, pine root,
melting with the winter, encountering
nitrates, bedrock, continent. Here native

bones and memories have since become vast
auctioned clearings, reserves, old palisades
dismantled by the weather, foreign tribes,
foreign customs clutched around a cross

that hammers nail, splits wood, erects with stone
a settlement. Arched above coiled rivers,
generators, a universe expands
indifference. Beneath the asphalt street

and concrete buildings, eons of boiled rock
imagine in tectonic sleep mitosis
still dividing. The weed admits the garden.
The icy road may be inclined to murder.

Thirst

Can the straw exceed the vision of the glass?
What beyond its culvert comes to pass?
The drinker learns an attitude, no more —
the glass as else when drained as just before,
and the straw, towering toward taste buds,
brings two together, human and the wild
periphery, there, outside any god's
trajectory, unreconciled.

Mr. and Mrs. Bklackburn Hamlet

Go upstairs
now your day

is done. Kiss your love
to dreamlessness.

Ignore the enigmatic
glare of the digital

clock on your bedside table; ignore the pacing

silence of the room; the
furniture: a sweater heaped

on a chair
is different

at night.

NEW OTTAWA POETS — Richard Carter

Downstairs
the seventies radio with dust on top

starts a seven-hour
shift; the fridge coughs, the naked sink

shivers under the tap
and knives and forks shine

in undiscovered light. Out the window,
above the primary school, the moon

marks the sky like a satellite
dish in a cosmos of plastic

wrappers that once were stars.

Things

I wish I had more courage, but being shy
I let all seasons briskly pass me by
and learn of them no more than if a book
between my fingers showed me every nook
arresting for sincerity and scope

and I remembered little, since my mind
scuttles all conviction that this rope
of blood once circled. For rarely can I find
a clarity to clean perception new —

apple, backyard birches, sun-parked car,
a fence-top squirrel's scramble, seem in lieu
of something else. What waits for us in things?
What careless whim drops motion into rings
widening to apple, asphalt, star?

Founder

The gantry hauls a crate into the air
that high above the ship seems to belong there
suspended in an always on the brink
before it lowers into life and talk
unadvertised.
    An unmoored ship may sink.
Some do. The floating splinters by the rocks
will bob with wave and foam. The bodies wash
ashore; they are not frightened that the sea
survived the small encounter; nor did they
hate the breeze that baffled thought away
so simply, snapping gyroscopes, deck awash
with mariners and motion.
    Such sally
alone grows calm with ocean: they weren't numb,
those dead, but buried in their hearts grew dumb
with love for what they saw, until a squall
requited tenderness, and gathered all.

Voice

I want to know
that a voice is.
I want to speak something

green with my hands.
I have two feet to mark
the ground, and eager
   thoughts
murmur in my wrists. I must make something

grow from this pavement
that the cars run over.
I want to draw
the blinds each morning
and hear my voice
   giving birth

to birds. I want this autumn
everywhere,
reddening the apples,
knocking on the doors of apartments.

I want to see
a swinging day
bright on the floor of an empty room.

I want to know
there's more than sunlight
holding dust there.

accountant

In the garden there the tree
is doing the accounts
untroubled. What light
may pass through such careful
boughs is filtered
slowly, the warmth
gleaned and understood by
every leaf
that grows. Rain, too, will
never be forgotten by
the darkened bark
or beaded leaf, on which the
scratching twig takes note
of rhythm in the worn street,
or the rattle of a garage
that opens, as a flower
opens, as a mouth must.

NEW OTTAWA POETS

Laurie Fuhr

Laurie Fuhr is a student at Carleton University, Ottawa. Her poems have appeared in *Bywords*, *Alter Vox*, *Graffito*, and Carleton's student newspaper, *The Charletan*. She has three chapbooks — *Newsprint Butterflies* (Phobe Press, 1998), *accident : a chain reaction* (above/ground press, 1999) and *asleep at the real* (Birdcage Books, 2000). The editor of *Blue Moon*, Ottawa's bimonthly poetry, art and fiction zine, Laurie hopes to make a difference in the Ottawa poetry scene.

shallow

I am stained
for all the wrong reasons —
you spilled yourself over me
w/out a thought
for the marks you'd leave behind.

you have a summerhome in
my dreamland, where everything
is black and white. last night
we chased newsprint butterflies
and the sky was blue as I was

when I knelt to catch you
a little extra beauty
and tore her wings.

this is a love that steals
from my heart and all the rest of me,
from my days and from my sleep:

I wake up
to a kind of ink
that won't wash off.

NEW OTTAWA POETS — Laurie Fuhr

mind's exercise

for Pat Davis, 1998

    pretend for a moment that I am beautiful
    that my sudden dove eyes broadcast
    at your frequency
    that my conjured dark hair is as long
    and slow as midnight rain —
    that my lips invite you as wine to a thirsty man,
    poisonous and cold and lovely

        or pretend that I am precious, fresh glass blown
        with the delicate fire of a soul life conspired to preserve,
        pretend that your hands are suddenly soft at the thought
        of a touch and careful at the thought to implement;

now pretend the light reflected now in my eyes
from this ruddy glowing room
once escaped from the tiny fissures in your heart,
slept in the air, and then seeped into my skin
as I one day passed by   to settle in my core and
there radiate, calling your name in beacon syllables

        but if these things are as difficult to picture
        as they are for me to become, then

pretend, finally, that I am simply a person
unlike any other
you have ever met before;
and in that simple mystery know
that if I am not inside your heart
I belong only in my dreams
where I could be anything —

        a bird flapping mad amber wings
        away from death —

SHADOWY TECHNICIANS

and if you can see this one thing
I'll imagine us children
and beg you to play house with me

NEW OTTAWA POETS   Laurie Fuhr

Witness

How often do I move
through this body
like a stranger

Whose arms are these
that are always open
for business

Whose fingers are these
that poke the sky
to make stars

Whose lips are these
that taught Georgy Porgy a lesson
(underneath the jungle gym)

Whose stomach is this
that bellyflops before sex and exams

Whose voice is this
that quavers
in the morning

Whose ears are these
that can't hear you whisper
in the dark

I am interrogating suspects
in someone's right eye
as we speak

It Must be the End of the World, Because...

We have almost exhausted Language.
We are running out of names for new cars
and words for love. Our children are called
for their grandparents, their children
are called for flowers, flowers
are forgetting their tongues.
Too many generations of Hibiscus
have gone by to remember what Eve
had named them.
We have used up every last word
in a Brand Name. We have more often
patented goddesses than we have told
their stories. We have trademarked
Monet and Van Gogh.
Every word for wonder has become
a curse. There are no more forbidden
words — no fear or respect for Language,
older than as many ancestors as we
can remember, because Language Is
Remembering. We are wasting
it, and like other natural resources,
it will soon be gone. Soon
we will only be able to speak
in caveman grunts
and clubstyle violence. Soon
Life will renew itself and
start again.

**The Shaky Hand of
Western Poetry**

In China, he said, the poets
are artists of both word
and canvass —

intricacy of alphabet
the brush letters are
as art themselves.
pictures in one form
make pictures in the other
come natural.

The shaky hand of
Western poetry
paints cactus and tumbleweed
where they ought not to be:
winter scenes, downtown
Calgary, the cowboy's
bedroom.

The shaky hand of
Western poetry
lets the convulsions of
a pick-up on a bumpy road
write pen on paper for it
when it tires

The shaky hand of
Western poetry
has fingers tall
as grain elevators,
a stampede of knuckles
drumming on the dinner table,
tiny cowboy hats where the rings
of fingerprints should be

SHADOWY TECHNICIANS

The shaky hand of
Western poetry
draws with the smooth
hand of China
at high noon

the merqueen's parlour

When I submerge from sleep,
I gasp for air because I
have been caught below the surface
of a dream for so long.
The temperature this close
to the sun is sudden incredible
heat. The tapestry on your wall
presents a portal, turning slowly
counter-clockwise, threatening
to whirlpool us in. From it,
I can look back into the ocean
of sleep from which I have visited
the rivers of dream. Let me
steer this bedroom starcraft
part the most menacing of meteor
showers and coral reefs —
to the merqueen's parlour we will
go for tea, bearing gifts of story
and song for her amusement

Old Man Moriarty

Damn that old
boxcar sunrise,
more beautiful than
in any picture-window
except a-way too bright
so's you can't see nothing,
double nothing since you've
been drinking.
Last night's bottle remnants
make a good mouthwash,
and a good pick-me-up too.

NEW OTTAWA POETS   Laurie Fuhr

Wired In

He sets his glasses down
on the dinner table
so he can see better
and they can see better.
What each of them see
they will tell the other
when wire and flesh
have been made
one again.

Pride

for David Collins

Sitting on the couch in
his Studio,
still proudly sporting
all his bony knuckles,
he tells me:
I have Irish blood
and am related
to the Last-Ever
     Bare-Fisted
Heavyweight Champion
of the World.

I picture the grizzled
old fighter
sitting on the couch in
his cold-water flat,
still proudly sporting
all his favourite scars,
telling a friend:
I am related
to the First-Ever
     Non-Violent
Irish Poet
in the World.

accident:
     a chain reaction

no way to describe
the fury scream
of car impact:
metal-on-metal-on-
concrete-on-bone
except
louder-than-loud

—

and every time you greet Death
as though flashing headlights
at an unlit sedan
on a midnight highway,

as though catching a glimpse
of his dark eyes
as you pass,

you will hear and feel
that fury again
and it will wreck you

—

a night goes by,
an average day except
I thought the sound had left me
in the whereabouts
of a Ron Sexsmith song
at breakfast.

but it was only hiding,
travelling in my bones and
       excavating marrow.

SHADOWY TECHNICIANS

I imagine myself moving
without skin,
without muscle,
I feel a tired unaccounted for
as though the sound is corroding
my blood,

    it is rusting me out —
    like a junkyard wreck,
    it has a story to tell

    of all the victims
of all the crashes

that ever made
that sound

—

two days later
the sound comes again
in the showerhead squeal
and again with the scrape
of a knife on a plate

    in the diner I went to
    to escape the refrigerator
    that kept mocking the sound
    in its sudden workings

and the creep call of crows
outside your balcony window

and the creak of the front door
as you headed off
to work.

aside from that,
I think the sound

NEW OTTAWA POETS — Laurie Fuhr

has gone back
where it came from.

    aside from that

NEW OTTAWA POETS

Robin Hannah

photo by Sean O'Neil

Robin Hannah is a native Torontonian, an honorary Haligonian, and for several years now a happy Ottawan. A chapbook *Line of Half* (above/ground press) came out in 1996, followed by her New Muse Award book *gift of screws* (Broken Jaw Press) in 1997. Her work has appeared in *Bywords, Hook & Ladder, Missing Jacket, Graffito: the poetry poster* and on the *Bard Reading Series* cassette. She likes to keep a low profile, and realizes this impairs her marketability.

**Indulgence
or, off with her head!**

Come come no need now
for violence cluck cluck
a simple cheque will do a largish cheque
we'll gently tender coolly palm
for you

to make bastards of your sons
a tinkling moneybag to nullify
to hell with the old wife!
and light the way
for the new
and improved
the church is sated
the slate is clean
the wedding pure
I say!
capital idea

NEW OTTAWA POETS   Robin Hannah

Crossbow on Argyle

November colourless

hangs over the street, heel-clicking stark
and stone cold

autumn lies dead by the curb.

She walks this morning, her breath
leaving clouds, like possibilities
and forgets to be afraid

nearby hate is cocked
and he is waiting.

The encounter comes quick, he knows what he wants,
a finger released and he's done

she leaves a stain
clotted cold across the pavement

a poppy-smeared reminder of the day.

(Crown Attorney slain by ex-spouse, 1991)

December 25 '91 — The Big Panic

The days have blurred the nights
have done the same there was Christmas
somewhere sandwiched in this family love and pain.

suddenly men at the door

and a stretcher steel and orange
canoed through the room and over the presents
candles blew out
while the adults stood about and stunned
clutched the handles of their holly eggnog mugs

the cries from a mouth dry with terror
I don't want to die mum I don't want to die
don't be silly, whispered back, don't be silly
don't be sad

death himself — paralysis
from the feet slowly up to the throat

and dad the missing piece arrives
trenchcoated knight
strides through and with a squeeze of his hand
knows it's all right
in the mind.

NEW OTTAWA POETS   Robin Hannah

The River Groove

The river groove, along and down
the Ottawa
from Mattawa

the river groove, les voyageurs
the leaving shore
the way

in the river groove, meandering
means meandering, means a seeing
from the side

the mirrored ways, the ambling
to a slowly coming widening
on the wind

the growing smooth, the drifting wood
the moves of all things permanent
rising wake

the river groove, a loosening
in August and in love
the sweating naked

the river groove, the greediness
of trees to water's edge
the waterfalls

the ceaseless and the subtle
goings from beginnings
beginning from an end

the river groove, the twilight
of a finely fallen sun
the water stills

to urgence, finely tuned
boozing to the soothing
darkened groove

the river groove, the music
sleeping slowly to the soul
the whispered lap

the misted path, the dawning seen
scent of time unanchored
swirling twig

the river groove, the being
understated, eddied, gently purposed
in the groove

the river groove, the feeling
like the river full and riverly
just that

riverly and full

NEW OTTAWA POETS

Robin Hannah

Pubic awareness activities
or, sex with ex and why

the endlessly soft cheek of first love
you seek out and tender your own cheek to meet it
close your eyes and the better to scent it
keep them closed

if it happens to happen say in February
that you happen upon it again in the dead,
in the dead heart of winter
and booze abounds

     around you swirls the past, a merry haze,
     smoky strangers, your two smiles

what you will find is it hurts
it receives and enfolds you like calfskin,
as mellow as mellow, as warm as the known to the bone,
but it will hurt

the way only February can, sandpaper
in frigid fucking dragged across façade
you'll find yourself rawed, and all over
ruddied hell

but when it's all over you're done
no ifs or rebuts to what's happened
sated, with a face softly toughened
nap-roughened, you simply wipe smooth

(for G. L.)

SHADOWY TECHNICIANS

A fair bit and well worth it

Some time soon after sunset
in the mistyrious way of the water
in the treeliest of seasons
we met

and come morning our two bodies
pools quiescent now seeking not to be
and to the swaying of those trees green and strong
began the journey

began the slow exquisite fall
from slowly it begins to slowly gather
whisper
of a glisten
of a quicken to a flow
to a murmur of converging
to the hum of summers rising
to our depths and swelling to our reach
and lappening our form and deepened our run
and rockied our paths and thrawny our way we keep falling
waving to hosannas sailing on
until we see

stir become tidal, ways become one,
scent become sung, and life horizon

her relations with scent

is it the same life she wonders same with life
her relationship with scent and she wonders

she remembers the funky sweat of her
up from her wide-opened cardigan
her nakedness inside, waiting at her desk and frosty window
she remembers a walk in the woods
in the wilds of July and shedding to her skin and smiling there
with smiling
she remembers moss in fall
its green surprise of plump while all else wizens
and an odour out of this world
she remembers twigs in April
the way they hold out their hands their new little hands
scented so strong from what's coming
she wonders what time does to what

yearnings that seem like forever
surelys that swear to go on
absolutes and so absolutely
singings that go singing off

instead she turns to her lover
her lover of now and not then
and then smiling
trails her hand inside his thighs and scents her fingers
licks her way up his chest expanse of skin
places gently places all of her odours on his
softly takes his mouth and smells winter

SHADOWY TECHNICIANS

peace tower scaffolded

silent for so long
who knows where the sound
has gone now
far underground

shielded stone face in repair eyes enclosed

so soon now soon
revealed to sound anew
and far richer
deeper for it

NEW OTTAWA POETS

Robin Hannah

Love in a cemetery

The scene is so serene
but it was pouring

it was summer
and the green rampant through the Gatineau Hills

and there among the strangers
we had planned to disrobe to the sun

we were beckoned on to see it through
the headstones grew grayer soaked on, the branches blacker
the grass grew alarmingly green and the leaves proved a canopy
unprotective

but we came, we came to see it through, see and be
and though I knew things would never be the same
here at least
I went on, clutched on and looked up at the sky
raining down in my eyes and soaking through
skin on skin and limbs slippery
I looked up at the sky through the trees

came alive with the power of death in tandem
death in tandem with living little deaths
and connection beyond this mortal soil

being at cottage

As the breeze comes
and the glass catches sky and ripples its blue into motion
and the shore stands afar furred in russet
and the birds flutter busy
and a wisp of a web catches sunlight
and the moss and dampened leaves soften into place
a softened path the last of the insects still wander
she wonders

feels her heart, catch
her marrow stir
her throat open

I love you
she says
and listens

NEW OTTAWA POETS   Robin Hannah

Oh to whistle

down a ladder
from under the road
comes a tune

man down a manhole in March
and suddenly my heart
feels like June

zen (TRIPLE WORD SCORE)

In my grottic atty, basemented
I make endless words of endless tiles
Of endless letters for nothing.

Jim Larwill

Jim Larwill has worked as an air-cooled engine mechanic, an electronics sheet metal fabricator, carpenter, janitor, property maintenance worker, home daycare worker, as well being a primary caregiver for eleven years. He is an Ottawa native and founder of the Omnigothic Neofuturist Writing Workshop. He has written plays and has been published in several chapbooks including *Old Growth* (Canadian Shield), *My Moist Red Tongue* (Canadian Shield), *Rock Video Love* (Canadian Shield) and *Rag Doll* (birdcage books). His poetry and fiction has appeared in journals such as *The Carleton Arts Review*, *Queen Street Quarterly*, *Missing Jacket*, *Bywords*, and *Blue Moon*. His poetry is also featured in *SPEAK!: Six Omnigothic Neofuturists* (1997, Broken Jaw Press). Jim is the proud father of three men.

Flipping the Double Helix Coin

Heart was target
    last time
Mayakovsky loaded his gun
    six shells
each one a small prayer
    the word turned bullet
and the trigger discovered
    an already known secret.

Red Square pigeons
    shit white
on tons of bronze
    hollow echo,
this blood stained page
    wrapped around
my own thin wrist
    curse pleading
death to stop
    knowing it never will
and I thank accidental God
    not abortive gun.

Poetry like mining
    radium
years for just one ounce
    critical mass
of nuclear thought,
    when I do it
more than a room
    splatters
my words not soldiers marching
    but children dancing.

I watch them grow famous
    spinning into unknown future
as my maiden tongue
    caresses curl of her ear.

Post-Modern Ljóσaháttur

Blue coated woman
rakes broken leaves
in scarf blown street.

She sweeps spiral dust;
fallen death fragments,
wind pregnant with winter.

Trauma

you try to paint a wall blank with water

you are blamed for the horrible pictures you have drawn

the images are indelible — sensations vivid

a memory with no context — dream you cannot scream free from

even you do not believe
or want to hear the story
you repeat
over
and
over

NEW OTTAWA POETS   Jim Larwill

Kiss

soft and cooing
she tastes as sweet as she sounds
slip of liquid velvet
on to my lips
tongue laps music
ears pulse
smell of burning honey

Reflection

They say the genius of Van Gogh was he
could make everyday unseen things seen;
like an old pair of workboots painted with
points of colour.

Now I stand naked over a mirror, my legs
wide apart. As I look down I am lost for words,
discover, I am not a genius, or very original.

I pull on my pants and go to the other room,
drag out my 15 year old workboots. Disappointed

    I begin a poem about

 scarred   and   holes.

   leather muddy

Broken Heart

When she phoned to cancel our first dinner engagement I said she had broken my heart.

"Not very original," she replied.

It was the third time she had heard it that day. I was not surprised, or threatened. The other two had probably meant it.

She asked if I loved her. She said too much light surrounded me — and the sparks:

"Always these sparks."

I laughed and said I thought she was the one in love with me.

We did not go out to dinner that night. Instead, I celebrated my birthday alone, sat up in my room with a twenty year old Bolivar, watched it soak up cheap Niagara Wine.

I smiled and smoked — the Cuban fumes taking me back to Havana nights. Taking me to soft Russian lips. The hot nicotine — mad razors on my tongue.

NEUTRAL GROUND

When I was younger
if I asked a girl out for a coffee,
there was sort of a unwritten understanding
that when we were at the Chinese Food Place
we wouldn't suddenly be fucking
upon cold tile floors, broken
plates of chow mein smeared by bodies
amidst the staccato of Canton curses.

Back then I thought people were
flowers, my heart — a root,
not a speeding car on
death ice streets hitting
every pedestrian possible.

When the coffee was finished
conversation would shift
to making love instead of war,
hands would meet, would lead
soft feet through bearded fields.

The touching, not a parking lot conquest
of violent crush lust, kisses — not
burning or desperate, when sex was a tender
neutral ground — not claiming to be love.

This Spring I Heard the Harmonious Clapping of Hands

Spring is a kind of death
   when water runs down to the sea
   flood gates wide open
   releasing six months
   of stagnant waiting
   the hog's back foaming with anger
when even spring is a kind of death
   and the sun murders white innocence
   drives it hard through
   the folded thighs of a fault line
   an arrow head of shale
   alone pointing defiant
   out of the broken crust of earth
   its delicate layers of rock
   lost in the whirlpool lather
when spring is a kind of death
   up out of this gorge
   the rush of air
   knifes as stale as fog in a graveyard
   cold and clinging to the surface of a breath
when even spring is a kind of death
   and this eye's fire drowns
   in the turbulent wrinkles
   a fragmenting mind
   each thought's electricity
   short circuited
when spring is a kind of death
   one that releases a river
   into a tirade
   every whitecap billowing a curse
   against a land frozen forever waiting
   the contorted winter of stagnant monsters
   aswim in our icicle memories
   the time when even these sediment cliffs
   rolled like waves
   the inland sea too warm to deny

SHADOWY TECHNICIANS

even spring is a kind of death
   and on the concrete weir
   running next to the bridge
   valley piles of square timbers
   no longer stacked like beaver pelts
   one on top of the other into a damn
   instead the empty slots below
   now arush with static absence
   wooden logs no longer covered with
   the green slick of slime
   but laced with a shatter
   of crumbling shells
when spring is a kind of death
   zebra mussels cling
   to cement pylons
   unaffected by the sermonic roar
   but also slowly eating bit by bite
   the concrete verses supporting
   this bridge and its traffic
when spring is a kind of death
   the literature of this stream
   turns back in on its self
   swallows great wave gulps of air
   explodes with a thundering
   acid hiss of bubbles spraying
   the face of a season with lies
   because this landscape will burst
   into a bitter melting of flames
when spring becomes a kind of death
   transforms the worm brown river
   into the twisting of a serpent
   one shedding its third and final skin
   as she opens her mouth
   swallows history whole
   blows away the banks
when spring is a kind of death
   and the world breaks
   into apocalyptic applause.

Trilobite Laughter

Today the rapid's roar
        reduces background static
                down to sobs

blackbirds curse the heat
        and a lethargic river
                darts with red flashes

I sit on regular rows
        trilobite
            inscribed shale

the rusting railway bridge
        fascinating me more
           than the hanging silence
                  of seagulls

steel rails on wood
        wood on iron
           iron on scum-licked stone

dark creosote ties
        laid like corpses
                along iron plates

rivets
    geometric shapes
            a lace work of crosses

woven between
                tombstone   pillars

steel rails on wood
        wood on iron
           iron on scum-licked stone

SHADOWY TECHNICIANS

each layer showing
        material division
                and the hand of man

farther downstream
        under construction
                a highway

it floats on
      steel scaffolding
              has no harsh beauty

strength of structure
        hidden
                as if by magic

steel rails on wood
        wood on iron
             iron on scum-licked stone

freight train passes
      mammoth box cars wobble
              a dinosaur rumble

fragmenting bedrock
            percolates
              with the sardonic laughter
                      of trilobites

I Whisper Love

I whisper love into your ear with the cool
    breath of spring as nestling feathers
    tickle your neck.

I whisper love with a forked tongue and
    cold blooded words that slice like a
    razor at the trunk of a tree, carving
    the bark away bit by bit in the hope
    of freeing you with a heart.

I whisper love as I crawl out of my skin
    only to tie it in a rubbing knot
    before spinning it down the drain.

I whisper love when a small hand pulls my
    finger, and I look down into the eyes
    of a child holding a plastic
    skeleton, her body little more than a
    battleground for cancer and chemotherapy,
    her Halloween smile mocking death
    and my own fear of life.

I whisper love past the velvet leaves of
    your naked seeing self with a prayer
    that forces its way into your womb
    where I hope to bind one love with
    another.

I whisper love across the graveyards of
    children into the dry eyes of
    grieving mothers who stand upon a
    world without divinity.

SHADOWY TECHNICIANS

I whisper love in the late night as I read
    the sonnets of Shakespeare, my tears
    punctuating his vain hope to
    resurrect his son with words as I
    slap the face of intellectuals who
    mediate poets in the same way
    scientists mediate the word of God.

I whisper love as I walk across a bloodless
    pond where you discover the twisted
    and dismembered arteries of a stump
    sinking deeper and deeper into the
    willowed mud.

I whisper love as I think of Mayakovsky and
    his love for Lili Brik and how that
    love turned into a bullet that in an
    instant ate through his heart, this
    same worm that now daily chews its
    way deeper and deeper into the frozen
    wood of my chest.

I whisper love now knowing that the
    vibrations of my own shouting voice
    tore the leaves from the trees and
    covered the world in a blanket of
    white regrets.

I whisper love in the hope that all I have
    preserved with ice and anger will one
    day thaw and will bloom into the
    light again.

I whisper love when I run my finger over
    the fruit of your decaying lips,
    their shape seeming to explain all of
    my life and future existence.

NEW OTTAWA POETS

I whisper love when my semen becomes lost
    and confused, attacked in the dark by
    the predatory words lying deep in the
    virile crevices of our fleshy
    membranes.

I whisper love to you my love in all the
    silent cells of your body, my melting
    marrow, an empty caress of wrinkles
    where I carve an epitaph with the
    fiction of my peeling skin, as small
    flakes are swallowed into the
    termination of a puffing wind.

Clare Latremouille

Clare Latremouille is a displaced British Columbian, originally from Kamloops. She is returned to the east after a ten-year haitus, and her work has appeared in various forms and places, including *Hostbox*, *paperplates*, *Missing Jacket*, *STANZAS*, the anthology *Written in the Skin* (1998, Insomniac Press), & the chapbook *I will write a poem for you. Now*: (1995, above/ground press). She is currently working on a novel.

schedule

the work you go to
every every and the bus and the ride and the corners you must stand
on waiting for something
else
in this cold dark morning full of mud and other lies
lost dog running in city street rain, digging in invisible mud
nothing else
to do besides bury yourself in the yard like an old
dog old dirty dog with cars wagging
dodging cars splashing wet dripping
all the
old children swimming for the top dogpaddling
all-over mud
crawling the surface still waiting
too old to play now standing full of children
tied to your streetcorner not watching the sky tearing down at your
clothing
all grown up your watch
your little skin and bones
buried
in yards somewhere away
child covered branches no girls allowed
the day you once had
grown over
new hair growing in
white and shedding like a dog

NEW OTTAWA POETS — Clare Latremouille

cave drawing

here is a book of poems that do not rhyme, that do not speak
here are pictures in iambic pentameter,
here is Mr Macleod,
here are all the ones we loved here the top-sided dog,
here the ones we lost
here the ones we do not know anymore,
that we never knew

here I will steal your love letters and make them my own
here I will write history in reverse,
here I will make sense of even nothing
here I will play until I am exhausted and I will not go back until I
am done
here I will write page three thousand and never be done
here I will place the pages in order and then fly them around the room
here I will make you out of words no one can see,
fighting under the surface of my skin

here is somewhere else you are not allowed to enter
here is my body here is the lamb of god who is everywhere
here are the lovers, stretched out behind like accidents
here are secrets, here are not secrets,
only skin passing down murderous visions
and I will be god
here I will make love to them
I will have sex with them I will fuck them right here on the floor
here I will force them,
I will take them until my flesh is dead

here are the same places gone quiet

here is you slipping back into air
here is this skin that you do not want
here is the word fuck by itself

here are the lovers no one can hold

SHADOWY TECHNICIANS

here is the picture you could not throw
here is the small baby you were, standing with your mother
here is me in the same picture, hidden deep within your skin,
breathing the same breath

here is your next birthday you will never have
here is the cake that will never fall into the ground
here is the breath I will press from my mouth to yours

here are you writing my lines for me in darkness
always two:fifty-two December the thirteenth
Tuesday and nothing after the same two:fifty-two and nothing after
here is your death certificate
rolled on all the walls over windows,
here is the little room where the heavens
began to disappear into screaming
here is help me help
me somebody oh god somebody help me can't somebody can't
breathe can't
breathe

here is the song here is always the song
sometimes in the night alone
sometimes in the night alone
pictures on the walls in blood and red earth

we remain by the fire small eyes watching

NEW OTTAWA POETS — Clare Latremouille

of eternity

*look into the sun of eternity
and let the shadows fall behind;*

this is what I found,
in my mothers belongings a small poem
a prayer more
than the tremor that begins somewhere in helpless
sinking to the base
passing the smell of your hot desert back
in places without skin, places deep
the night gone like summer gone into
eternity, more skin than I could hold
this air this rag I wear
all left of you
another voice at the end of your line
this sickness I let penetrate
nothing here nothing real

in the shadows you are the lover
without love
you are the cigarettes we lit,
the empty bottles of every description,
the green growing dishes in the sink,
the pain in your empty back, the soft of your kiss walking away
that can never feel the caress of words
meant to cut

in the shadows you are the lover
something to lie for

in charge of only nothing even my own skin betrays me flush
at the sound of you in another voice,
the laugh of you

escaping into the noonday street

SHADOWY TECHNICIANS

something to die for
besides being dead

NEW OTTAWA POETS

theories on the human animal

but

if pain were enough

for us we would not

be eating stolen green beans

at four in the morning

in your dead grandmother's bed

which we are

which we are

SHADOWY TECHNICIANS

**in which
we discuss the passage rites of manhood**

I will not trouble you with lies only I will make the truth so
painful you will be forced to desire the erotic sounds of my
storytelling

I will wrap my legs around your imagination. I will not be
flesh, I will lick you until you scream this is what you will
tell yourself

I will make my eyes green, I will make you even more beautiful
than I am, I will stare at you until you are forced
to confess

this holy night this gentle talk
we string christmas lights candlelights in darkness we are both
too alone for this frail faithfulness, this child game,
arms touch by accident and bristle, reflex, we will
lose this game

in this late hour I have become the last one
on the face of the earth even now we are dissolving
into fable

NEW OTTAWA POETS — Clare Latremouille

d. June 17, 1989

nevermore
in these walls
sounds of leftover potatoes and turnips emptied
into old cottage cheese containers, clink of spoon
against pot with chipped lid
you will not pass gas in surprise at the sink,
there will be no bread to put back from
the place, no almost not used napkins to fold for your
drink of apricot brandy
makeshift coaster, you will not snore
while I wash the two dishes and five glasses and one
pot and a pan and a steamer and a perfectly good piece of plastic wrap
with a scraper you made yourself out of onion bags and you
watch *The Nature of Things* and I
turn on the little light at the table while you sleep and
look at your lists and bottles of useless pills around your placemat like
worldly treasures like nuts around a squirrel
reflecting in the shimmer of the freshly wiped
arbourite and
I stare at the gardening magazines and *Catholic*
Digests on your shelf
and wish there were no
CBC no wax images of cats with marbles for eyes no amaryllis plants
with Christmas shiny paper from last year no address books full
of relatives you will never meet and god
so bored staring out out out
seventeen-year-old legs and eyes and breasts leaning out
the front door until you
waking snort and hair all tipsy and another little shot and the
cribbage board in pyjamas and smack the deck and fifteen two and
four and a pair is
us
and what was it like when and what did you do and do
you remember and finally
to bed to bed with no teeth face all shiny to kiss
goodnight waiting in my next little room
for one more breath one more after one
more pinching through the walls

d. December 13, 1977

Moon
Is cold
As me
Maybe from this stack of nothing I won't be
Utterly amazed at how dead you still are
Here is cats fighting, here is the moon twitching
Here is you still dead dead dead under cold
January
And the time it takes to scrape lies onto my own
Stories

You are just dreaming
With the snow angels
and I am growing
Your face

Clare Latremouille

riding hood

it is only the bathroom but I
flicker the light
consider infidelity

human sacrifice

this is where they found her
scraped and broken glass scraped and broken hands
rosewater mothersoft hands, broken on the floor
soft barefoot dirty I
open the bathroom cupboard and prepare to meet her,
ancestral crypt alive with flickering, empty skin alive, warm
still from your almost touch this is where they found her
florescent with enamel cleanser, sparkling whiter, skin colour
flashing harsh in the cupboard the swirl of hairpins rose blood
lipstick stiff and long gone already

back of hand unnatural red I try her on
seeking warm mother eyes in the faltering mirror
but these breasts are not yet cold,
in their white a shiver
passing through
like rosewater
soft sharp hands, scraped and broken eyes,
rosewater breasts

mother eyes alone in the reflection
mother eyes alone
my own black eyes waiting

hungry

wolves
eating each other alive
in the next room

Yalecom Valley

I have friends who walk around naked
where they live
even when they are not washing, or skinny dipping
which they often do on hot days, which the days often are
where they live, and anytime you walk or drive or
ride up on horseback
you may see them and each other
pale and not so pale
bobbing and leaning among the tomato plants, eating
toast and tea on the kitchen porch, waving
at you from the driveway with a hat
on and there is nothing strange about it except you
are unable to shed your image of yourself as
damaged somehow or wrong even
though you do not feel this about them
and they are just the
same as you only
without clothes

slumber party

The dare was almost always something to do with
taking off clothes I dare you
to streak down to the bottom of the driveway, I dare you
to pick a tulip from Muskolyk's yard I dare you to go all the way
to Mechem's house wearing only a blanket
naked underneath the ultimate risk even though
amongst ourselves bodies were examined and categorised with
scientific detachment: flat pink nipples and rounded bellies
of most except Kathy Overli curiously growing armpit hair and
sticky-out tits, and all of us skinny legs and chunky legs and
little bums and little bigger bums and even
the bare bummed penis and scrotum of Mark Mechem going pee
behind the utility shed, and it wasn't until Bobby Cross found
the box of *Penthouse* magazines in his garage that we found
we were being
sexual
and things changed
after that

SHADOWY TECHNICIANS

moving boxes

somehow we have all become
lovers after this
garage sale tumbling
together on the scattered mothers
and husbands
babies and hair and skin and tongues all colliding
lost letters from a box embedded
in our backs twisting
like blankets and here is your father and here
is mine and a girl you once
but that was a long time ago so is this
so long ago sweet so sleepy so
very very sleepy here I kiss
my husband
goodnight
in the soft warm space
between your back blades

try sleeping

try sleeping
you say
and I do
try
two:thirty in the morning and Elvis is not even awake
in this house of the most lively dead
but I am
dressed in your grandmothers lovers shirt do not be afraid I am
with you always even unto the end of the
night, moon like skintight flickering candle up and
gone, on her picture on the wall, ours
on the floor, do not be afraid
we are all perfect gentlemen, we are all human
bleeding somewhere underneath
her hand on mine warm, covered in wax
human remains
we are only
human and she is only someone we will not see
anymore, your hand in mine is colder

and I will miss you

we hold hands
and squeeze
in two

Garden

I can make
the garden grow, the sun fall up and down in the sky, a man
full grown from passion in my tissue, in secret
places I hide my fat and wait
for rain for rain for rain

Garden II

but
of all the flowers, I do not chose
yellow head like
suns for tiny worlds of aunts and bees and children
and they cannot live in the soft bed, they do not
smell nice and are crabby
when I die I want these blown over my dirt
like a prayer

Garden III

make a wish any wish
hold this picture of you
in my hand a princess a queen of the corn
with lupins and corn and kohlrabi
green green green a piece of paper joining this skin
to my own oh again again and the night is
all around the rustle of nets over strawberries, the starlings
are crying the garden gloves sleeping,
the shush shush of your garden shoes walking
towards the back porch door, ghosts
in the picture, rattle of the porch
door, dandelion stem
in my hand

Clare Latremouille

Garden IV

this is morning
sun wake you are dreaming a world
long gone sunrise draws water,
and the bird of morning on this day a thousand years old
digging in red clay in black mud in brown solid blood, here a seed, here
sweat to grow it, and twist of the green to touch the blue blue sky,
you cause the sun to rise in this way, pulling out of the earth
with your tiny woman's hands, pulling life
together from a thousand thousand days held
together across the grip of your tiny hands and the hunger for enough
to feed a thousand empty
children, falling from your hands like apple rolling to
seed, rolling into the centuries of dust and dirt and
mud, turning the sun, turning the earth, and
if you were not
here it would only be Wednesday in the backyard on Desmond road

Garden V

Now it is my turn
I stand over the plot of earth and consider how best to break it,
consider the tilt of the moon, the position of stars, the prevailing wind,
the flavour of the gods
I pick up a clod of earth hold it softly
in my teeth and swallow
it wholly, wholly, wholly

Gardening Tips

I ask you
now
it is too late of course you being
dead and over
three thousand miles away
anyway about the feeding of roses, blood red, domestic
I remember you said when you were in the convent the nuns
took the water for soaking menstrual rags
to feed strange and wonderful flowers raspberry heavy blood scent,
heaven sent
from the bodies of young girls and secret women
petals falling
shards of flesh earth
red with the blood of saints I ask you
the man at the story said bonemeal
is this your secret? a lump a breast a
leg a piece for us all
every year you got shorter and shorter

NEW OTTAWA POETS

Karen Massey

Karen Massey's poetry has appeared in various Canadian literary publications and in anthologies including *Written in the Skin* (Insomniac) and *Vintage 97/98* (Quarry) and her chapbook, *Bullet* (above/ground). She received an MA in English Literature (Creative Writing) from Concordia University and has been living in Ottawa since 1990, working as an artisan.

SHADOWY TECHNICIANS

In the Pub Named for the Irish Expat Writer We Idolized in School

You dare me across the table daring you. It's been years.
Our stories taunt, even your blue-tongued cigarette smoke
is eloquent tonight, shimmers cunningly

Years ago, in libraries, we tore off covers and ripped out pictures
of our true-to-life lives,
dumped the narrow drawers of memory's card catalogue
while everyone watched —
who could care?
We'd fall away to hallucinated dust,
like lovers tearing off one another's clothes,
hearts pulsing in our hands

Now we are *this close* — this serious transplant, sans all dark narcotics
We don't mention though it's painfully evident we both crave a blister-scarred past,
its defining edge undetectable in our serious, studious gazes;
we walk the streets in heavy boots that have fled yielding shadows
yet stood their ground when the knife wielding turned ugly,
the gouges too deep for Emergency
Who'd expect this of us today?
We've never even spoken
of this twisting world of our alliance,
this taboo secret life of *other* Right now I'm feeling gorgeous in plain sunlight
I'm in a reverie of how much Guinness we could have shared one night
just before the nightshift guard turfed us out and we'd stumble awkwardly through
not desire
not lust
but that truth captive
in the torn-cuticle ugliness, that safety in knowing
we walk upright in dark or light and cast a mere shadow of those former cells,
we're on *this* side of the law now, hands in pockets,
nails bitten to the quick That's it,

the vestigial remains of that precursor world,
fingertips raw with our antisocial habit:
it's the iron taste of blood, brute cockiness mixed with panic in the dark,
the pounding of footfall and heartbeats escaping danger and heading
down by the river,
drugs or money pumping ferocious in us like a disease,
like a pathogen gunning at its cure,
eradication

We bite our nails
None rival the extent we go to, they can't know
it's the taste of that other world we crave,
a pain we control,
Living writ large and torn off in small crescents,
blood pulsing painful beneath that surface

One bite till release and we both know it
and here we are being so unbelievably *good*,
absently thrumming fingertips on the stained table;
caged by white smiles, fluoride-strengthened

In the Kitchen With Some of Matisse's Women

We've been talking all morning,
taking advantage of winter light,
the philodendrons, some real, some scissor-cut paper
sway in the heat of discussion.

Freed from canvas, the women
stretch their arms and legs luxuriously as cats,
hold their teacups demurely
or not,
talk dirty with words red as Henri's pigments.
Clarisse, with her guitar, is surprisingly shy,
stretching long fingers over impossible chords.

Look at us: we're voluptuous, Madeleine exclaims.
No one can argue with these breasts,
identical pairs of firm, perfect rounds,
ripe as the apple on the side table.
These women are six feet of colour,
cartoon hairdos and rosy cheeks.

And what they don't say — not much —
finally released after being held by Henri's gaze,
frozen for sixty years.
I tell them what gossip I know of the fables of their families.
Dorette just sits quietly, tightening and relaxing her arm,
after reaching so long for that apple in the red room —
You looked as though you were polishing that apple,
Clarisse asserts, setting the guitar down,
scrutinizing her fingertip calluses.

All of this due to disagreement with Henri, you know.
He'd painted the red room blue at first,
despite my entreaties,
so to punish me, he left me at the table,
forever reaching for that sumptuous apple!

NEW OTTAWA POETS Karen Massey

Better off than Corinna, I add, *one of the women cast
by Henry Moore. She's big-hipped, but
headless —*

For the Stones In her Pockets

> *This is death, death, death she noted in the margin*
> *of her mind; when illusion fails.*
> — Virginia Woolf, Between the Acts

fragile words are the woman
delicate inside her body
holding its secret captive over fifty years
filling her head with the wet sand of madness
she cannot climb out of its night
will not turn down the thick blankets of grief

like thrush eggs smooth inside her dress pockets
she carries brown speckled stones
to counteract the water's buoyancy
the stones are growing
are swelling with her life's heaviness
soon they burst the pocket seams
of her underwater skin

Virginia drowning off-stage like Ophelia
the silent weight of stone
drawing her down to muddy death
through decades of brilliant testimony
caught fluttering in pages

giant stones deliver her

NEW OTTAWA POETS — Karen Massey

Sylvia Plath in Heaven Does Tie-Dye

I have done it again.
With pigments permanent as death, I've managed
To undercut heaven's hygienic white. Soon all poets
Will career through glitterless clouds in rainbow robes,
A tie-dyed riot of poets:
Here comes Homer on Sappho's arm,
Don't my colours reflect their epic charm?

O poppy red, turquoise and tangerine,
Inky hues from spinach to indigo,
Juice of sweet-tart berries, all beautiful stains,
Bright as a cancer cell, as crow's eye;
When I'm through there'll be cacophony,
Dull stars will wink amazed from their marquee.

You ask, and I'll gladly admit:
Dyeing
Is an art, like everything else.
I do it exceptionally well.

Behold this transcendent kitchen chemistry,
Measuring and mixing my fibre-reactive recipe,
This is my passion, mother-love, a lark!
Here is Mardi Gras in a vat, a tepid baptism of lilac or vermilion;
I'm one of Shakespeare's three weird sisters stirring her cauldron.

How satisfying is the unveiling, untying the resist,
Freeing lengths of cord wound like a tangled umbilicus,
Eyes anxious to discover how far the colour has migrated,
Cheery secrets moving furtively along damp pleats.
I complete each with an exacting touch,
With syringes of lemon dye, of orange and grape —
I administer colours pure as tastes.

SHADOWY TECHNICIANS

Yes, we all *would like to believe in tenderness:*
Mother-lips on a babe's sweet brow,
Orpheus plucking out our accompaniment, *sotto voce* —
How we long for that ecstatic kiss —

But what bright therapy, this daily tie-dye —
To cloak the poets in luscious garb.
Beginning with those closest to eternity,
I dye my way
                into your future.

(Italicised lines in first and third stanzas are from Sylvia Plath's poem, "Lady Lazarus" and from, "The Moon and the Yew Tree" in stanza six, first line.)

Whining Is No Longer Fashionable

To whine is no longer in vogue,
it sickens like cholera,
hammers rusted nails into the flesh.

Flesh has taken a beating lately.
Flesh of the heart.
Flesh has been abused.
The hammer, anvil, stirrup, even these
smallest bones of the human body
are sick to death of tapping the Morse alert.

Stop trying to build a better heart attack!
Forget the military applications, from a
human perspective,
all flesh and responding bones
have had it up to here with the pitiful whine.
State something useful, *quelque chose pratique!*
Now that we've managed

to take everything apart.
Perfected the technology of fission.

Act. Act of creation.
Go away with your quarks and neutrinos.
Give us this day our glorious cells.

Bullet

Finally my neighbour turns down his stereo,
Live BB King's blues fade to applause, six-stringed Lucille
is hasped into her leather case and the afternoon pauses
planning what to do next with its darkness,
cold November rain

Drowsing in the sitting room,
poetry book a colourful pup tent on my chest,
I listen to the hiss of tires on wet pavement,
feel the low rumble of the boiler heating water
which roils invisibly through plumbing,
stretches into seven apartments of radiators

My right hand traces the curve of my left breast,
deftly finds the small lump, like a bullet
caught beneath the thin surface of skin,
and though I know exactly where to feel for it, how to feel it,
I cannot fathom how I'm feeling *about* it,
this bullet sent from some unseen part of my body,
sent to frighten and incite,
mute missive I cannot cypher,
possible cyst, the doctor said, she cannot say
for certain, the mammogram
                  inconclusive, my breasts young and dense

My body continues to wring itself out with cycles,
is bleeding now, will bleed again and then
the diagnostic ultrasound,
                four more weeks to carry this question,
grenade I've lugged silently, staggering through late summer, early fall,
through breast cancer awareness month,
past survivor stories, past grieving lovers and families

I'm not married, I told the technician
leading me to the room where I disrobed for the mammogram,
she'd called me by my mother's name, *Mrs*,
her voice like whisky and music

She gently pressed a clear sticker over the lump:
X SPOT, within the O, a radiopaque bead,
dark referent on the X-ray

> *No children   no nipple discharge   negative family history*
> *thickening   asymmetry*   my sage doctor's jagged handwriting

Four more weeks to carry this bullet,
locked in tight as BB's Lucille in her velour-lined case
Like a child struggling to tote a heavy, precious guitar,
mindful of the music hushed inside

SHADOWY TECHNICIANS

Patients' Lounge: Day Surgery

Naked beneath generously-cut hospital cotton,
I enter the patients' lounge,
take a seat beside a woman likely 50 years my senior,
dressed in identical regulation chic. On my other side,
a man reads the first edition *Citizen*, striped flannel
pyjama bottoms giving a masculine edge to his gown and robe
combo. We're four women and two men, waiting,
supplicants wearing coded ID bracelets,
blue booties, elasticized at the ankle.

We're here with our documented bodies, our expectations,
with our abstinence from fluids and food since last evening;
we're scrubbed clean as per signed instruction sheets,
no make-up, no Rolexes, no jewellery.

Overhead the lounge TV flashes, through the ending
of *Canada A.M.*, through *Regis & Kathie Lee* live from Vegas,
we sit casually and too quietly,
biting our lips, pretending not to think,
attempting indifference to the procedures before us;
one woman is wrapped in a flannel blanket,
the scent of bleach and her nervous shivering
faintly discernible.

It's as if we came here in these identical suits and attitudes,
and we're waiting in this lounge
like we're waiting for a job interview
governing an important career move.

We feign interest in the television, in the glossy magazines
whose corners are slightly curled.
Some people make their money easily, the elderly woman beside me
shrugs, motioning toward the TV, a radiant sparkle in her eyes.
   I look up at the screen as Kathie Lee
   is carried on stage on a gilded stretcher
   and Regis is hoisted by turbaned women in glitz.

NEW OTTAWA POETS

Karen Massey

The patient's face looks so old and vital
I just want to hug her, I want to
tell her she looks beautiful in her simple dress, though all I
manage is a smile.

In the corridors, nurses come and go
like crepe-soled angels in cotton,
calling us away individually
to take temperatures and blood pressure readings,
to verify the nature of each surgery:
It's your left breast, correct?
Right. I mean, correct. I'm not nervous,
I'm looking forward to this procedure and pathology results,
to the truth at the end of a season
of bodily worry and medical technology.

Any minute now, one of us will be called
to enter the void of general anaesthetic,
where the sterile blade will be guided by the surgeon's hand
along the marking drawn on in pre-op.
Each unique and distinct procedure shall be conducted,
each body entered, looked into and redefined.
Tumours shall be excised,
atypical tissue will be removed,
just like that, on this Thursday morning;

painlessly opened and peered into
intimately,
and without memory,
then drawn closed by the knotted ends of sutures.

SHADOWY TECHNICIANS

Post Biopsy: Recovery Room

One by one,
wired to sensors and dizzy from morphine,
oxygen masks pressed against our faces,
sound and light breaking through until finally eyelids
lose their impossible weight,
we'll awaken
impatient for the surgeon's words

>I overhear two nurses whispering:
>*one patient won't be leaving today*

O sweet relief to hear the nurse assure,
No, no, dear, squeezing my hand; *you're going home this afternoon*

And then that spattering pathos thudding into my belly:
some other woman won't —

her diagnosis blasting into and through me
like buckshot fired down the scrubbed corridors
of this shifting dream of nurses
and slick and insufficient technology

NEW OTTAWA POETS — Karen Massey

Forbidden Words

i

We bit into their flesh with ripe pleasure,
hard consonants dripping snide slurs, our hard-cored nasty peaches of
    obloquy;
we'd peel off succulent diatribes with our puerile wit —
tongues engorged with descriptions of sex we couldn't have —
and dish out curses we pretended to comprehend
while elders, mortified by distaste for our disparaging words,
threatened to soap our mouths back to their angelic beginnings.
We were simply gluttonous with newfound diction.
All those tasty taboo terms
we'd heard them swallow back with beer and a wink to buddy on the barstool
dissolved into impossibly sinful talk for daughters
who'd giggle wide-eyed at our grandfather whispering, *For Christ's sake,*
just before his Sunday supper grace, *Amen*

ii

In our house, we dispelled the body's red mysteries
by speaking with correct terminology; we knew only Latin names
for Sunday school censored parts our classmates snickered over,
unwittingly tossing out euphemism, they were dispensing placebos —
our ace in the hole at any school yard orgy of slang: *uvula*.
In our house, facts paraded as facts;
numerous medical texts documented the body's stimulations and betrayals:
all of those terms skulking in tissue, effervescing in the bloodstream,
we viewed as labelled photomechanical reproductions in living colour.
To us, those blood-engorged words oddly forbidden to other kids
were no big deal —
they were simply a series of foreign terms — articulated sounds;
just so many velars and labial-dental fricatives —

NEW OTTAWA POETS

rob mclennan

rob mclennan is the author of over two dozen poetry chapbooks and four full collections of poetry, including *bury me deep in the green wood* (ECW), *Manitoba highway map* (Broken Jaw) and *The Richard Brautigan Ahhhhhhhhhhh* (Talonbooks), all published in 1999. The editor of *Written in the Skin* (Insomniac Press), a poetry anthology to raise money for AIDS charities, his 5th collection, *bagne, or, Criteria for Heaven* will appear with Broken Jaw Press in autumn 2000. The editor/publisher of *STANZAS* magazine and above/ground press, he won the CAA/Air Canada Prize in 1999 for most promising writer in Canada under 30. He is currently working on a long-poem, calld "hazelnut", and a novel, calld "Place". He lives & writes in Ottawa's Chinatown.

featherlite

        midnight, & the city shuts down a third day running.
chinatown is black, the whole span of eastern ontario
& western quebec 'a skating rink', as my father would say,
               & then he does.
        ive heard enough of el nino to know

theres something wrong, balmy days
     in calgary & burnaby flurries. ice leading the trees into
storybook pictures, a tale of a lonely queen w/ a cold heart
   & a little lost boy, searching

        for a way back home. branches
crackle like glass & my heart drops, tearing
   thru powerlines & parked cars, clawing at brick
& yr kitchen window. i slide home down the hill
      under flashes of blue, bursts
    of light & dark, explosions in the distance. all around,

    the sky burns, glowing. all around,
     the ground disappears. i bite my lower lip
  until i begin to taste blood, feel

electricity crackle in the air like a kiss.

sky, like a thesis (for kath macLean

you cant imagine what it starts w/
point a to point b poetics
just a car driving long in one direction

> & she says that photographs hold the same space as sound
> where memory tweaks & fallout blows
> the scent of a womans hair in the
> captions of a song

everything the body occupies the heart does
altho very few ever make that slight connection

> like a puzzle that fits, once you step back far enough
> & when it does, on forever, like a prairie, like a sky, goes

people & skyscrapers & waves (for claudia lapp

if there can ever be a list of everything
that can be listed, what little kids
     are smaller than

          the moon in the sky was only half last night
          astronomers in the know scan wild
          for where the rest got to, keeping quiet
              & out of the newspapers

if you could have me for free now would you
human attachment & sentiment both a
     help & a hindrance, some nights

          & continually begun again, cars halloween streetsigns
          70s songs remake on the radio
          & whether it matters if george washingtons tomb
              has *anyone* in it (including him)

my brother, ludwig (for jan zwicky

        in the end, im told, all that remain
are words. an old man taps his cane
   down bank street whistling
blue moon, & other
popular songs
   from between the wars. *tell them ive*

   had a wonderful life, he sighed, expired
finally at a later age, & inspiring
modes of thot & the philosophers song
for generations of true like minds.

      all that i know about the world
ive found in books, but only
   since my cables cut. goodbye cnn,
& my weekly *bleu nuit*. oh ludwig,
                i just cant go

for flavoured coffees, extra
shots of vanilla in my paper cup,
or the story of the boy
   who got scurvy in fruitland, b.c.,
eating only at mcdonalds,

morning, noon & night.

paraphrasing don mckay

                        there should always be a house
we never live in, michelle says, paraphrasing
    & perhaps even ruining, she worries.

listening is not the same
as learning, i know. a letter in the newspaper writes,
"you dont understand anything" & perhaps i never will.

       its nearly forty years since they flooded out
the st lawrence seaway, & my
ears are still ringing, putting
a whole community underwater. my exwifes father
part of the construction crew following orders.

he died a few years ago when his insides failed,
a genetic theme my daughter may have heard,
    like a musical note, sounding thru her too,
& wondering what the chances are.

when we drive the dirt roads over
the raisin river, all she wants to do
    is look at herself in the rearview,
see if cars are following,

suspicious of everyone, everything.

NEW OTTAWA POETS — rob mclennan

train

        maybe you know how to live.
            w/ stops in toronto,
buffalo, you talk of walking
                like marilyn,
    thru niagara falls. young men
      like barrels
           throwing themselves at you.

SHADOWY TECHNICIANS

ferry delay, terminal

            it makes such a case for staying home,
trees bent nearly double in the wind

                      this coffee gives me strange gas,
a flat hard bench all to myself

     this is not how i wanted
                to see vancouver

NEW OTTAWA POETS rob mclennan

death & death & other poems about origin

because we have to live w/ so much of it.
everybody knows. there are noises
& then there are places
      where there are none. the silences.

to come. the body breaks down
into quick turns of phrase & sweats
      down the shower drain like soap

by the water turnd cold from hot.
the obvious between breaking
      & bending. like the reed,

for instance.

from **bagne, or, Criteria for Heaven**

23. blowing a new day into a new season
fr lise downe

        never reaching the end,
miles of untended earth & fractured
    roman walls, the grander

human scale. like letters written,
never sent.

    for three hundred years they waited,
a line they dared anyone to cross

      but no-one did, the disinterested
barbarian hordes
& the occasional hole poked thru stone hearth.

rebuilding the world
          from the roman eye
      in the centuries after christ, this empire
            on the edge of forever

as hadrians wall, even fresh
      not fifty years later,
sat unoccupied,

    grown over w/ weeds,
& grazing

24. the other eye the final hieroglyph

fr gwendolyn macewen

        when you know there are no bounds,
symbols etched in flesh the only record

    & what the first eye
               tends to forget,
images of the secular & the end
                    of a sword, as sand dunes

        rise
          & fall
    w/ the same regularity
        & precision

whether we are here
or not. the other eye

    tracing a line between the sky
& the singular moon, digits
            of stars across the body
                  of heaven,
bright tattoos. at the moment these things were written,
interpreting lines on sunbaked clay,
    calling

        i am here
        i am in this place

    now

SHADOWY TECHNICIANS

29. winter when our minds fill up with snow

fr dennis cooley

              until were nearly obsessed with it
attitudes are inflexible things
    tight   on the cusp

suzanna moodie in a house somewhere north
far more north then,
        even if it were here

            as buildings creep higher
                  towards polar north
& bulldozers plough an eager path

the city of boston shut down
        at least once a year
      by the first hint of blowing snow

            ah, you silly americans, cold chorus

even as we cross wires, wrap our
      minds around sled dogs
           & pierre burton,
    sergent whatsisname of the mounted police,

        two months in twelve of bad skiing

31. and how we slowly began to look like her

fr linda rogers

        in the southern states,
the mirror'd hull
    of a government box
discolours in the form
of the virgin mary,
arcs
of oil & water
      nearly three storeys tall

        hundreds of believers appear
to pay homage,
pray
    as psychic hotlines go under
            in quebec & elsewhere
when no one saw it coming
the incredible jojo savard

        who says religion
              is a fading negative,
different articles of belief
    moving tenuous into the future, imperfect
                & unknown
& the desperation to find something
        to hold on to
          images of worry beads & other artifacts
          & my television tells me so it must be true

SHADOWY TECHNICIANS

35. japan in my own language

fr karen maccormack

          misunderstanding the dance,
the two step of honour, the rise of ambitions,
of *we who are about to die*

clouding over fragments of human nature
filaments burning as they flame
& everything else the taste of smoke

two scottish women over coffee
deconstruct the japanese perspective
from 1940s onward
old enough to be young
    during wwII
& missing out on their own eyes gloss

ive heard tell
      that westerners
can never comprehend buddhism
to truly understand
you have to be born
into it

   like monty python
to the french
a joke
you can never
explain

59. waiting for a rescue hours overdue

fr carmine starnino

      even buddhists
           have to come in
          from the rain,
              she says

NEW OTTAWA POETS

Ian Whistle

photo by W. Hood

Ian Whistle was born in Winnipeg in 1971, and divides his time between there and Nepean, Ontario. He edits/publishes the concrete/visual zine h&, & firsth&books. He is the author of two chapbooks — *apostrophe* (firsth&books) & *resemblances* (above/ground press).

remember by

you out there
listening   — the million-dollar pop song
following the news, bang pow

        — gives, it baby, gives
gave it wings and off it flew, let it
float out of my open fist

who knew, to enter
        the belly of the dragon
only to be shit out, left

steaming on the dance floor
,yesterdays news?

NEW OTTAWA POETS — Ian Whistle

light

words I am no longer using

      ~~time~~   ~~soft~~   ~~swiftly~~   ~~music~~

creative writ(h)ing told us to stay (away
    from abstracts) all
poets in their own (writes)

    ~~love~~
        bring me
concrete images, weigh that down

or this cemented poem pure hard
        things

(paperwork the next twenty years)

I ~~love~~:

    Belgian chocolates
    German wines
    C.S. Lewis
    a resolute sympathy for

down, good, down

Virginia slims

                over underground,
we're through. I don't know what got into you.
[scenery: we sleep. we remain.]

      skirt high over thighs,
fiction relates waves. bang.
[scenery: we sleep inside each other. you inside.
      she beside.]

               those feel-good cures.
one passed over, never meant.
[scenery: the problem from moment one.]

chances thin. no-one win.

NEW OTTAWA POETS   Ian Whistle

Virginia maple

[likely, frosted
                  [white legs]
            chicken-commercial, parts-are-parts-are
-parts-are-parts
                            stream/lined
gleaned and meaned   ]a hard time
                                   hitting you up for
   [tanned eyes]
                            knuckles, curved
[where your legs go dark]

                                  Winnipeg the
                                  pre-/post-
MODERN CITY. hit me up I'm lonely,

      I'm afraid.   (rescue me)

SHADOWY TECHNICIANS

there was no blood

                                        enough to talk about
                                        ]love
                                        and the human

          breaking glass   *lips*
               are red   with your beauty
          focus
          on you leaving

                                          not destination
                                          or the journey

thinking about point-of-origin
rooms discarded and already shifted

floors cleaned and new sheets
a hotel bar with my name on it

                                        perhaps
                                        perhaps not

                enough talk
                about life
                about redemption

                I'm waiting for something cataclysmic
                I've decided to wait to be reborn

NEW OTTAWA POETS — Ian Whistle

the seventh seal

] death and
  taxes and
    black costumes.   playing for your life
                                            has never been so real.
              a plague for your sins. (already happened.)

the
black
rot
      of stench, even
from a colourless reel, watching your back
                as it leaves your face. travelling

                        among
                the squares. king one,
over bishop. knight
after knight.   in the end, spy

with his third eye
    running, seven figures

        [dance from rocky caste
        along the thin curved line

and never escape from it at all.

SHADOWY TECHNICIANS

a bout de souffle (breathless)

] beware, jessica, movie posters
are not always
as they appear.   the shatterning mnemonics
                                   and where cigarettes.
                            [kisses match.

                one object
           reflecting, staccato gestures
                              an art of collage
and singling out a favourite moment.

                an uneasy
                relation
                to telling, fools
                          are a constant
                                  bedfellow.
                            a gentleman
from verona keeps calling, he will
    not leave. both ironic

and transformational.

NEW OTTAWA POETS   Ian Whistle

2 poems for Elvis

                      I park my boat   ] running,
                                            walking, or even
                                            kissing

        for a cure just isn't enough. pity meetings.
                the king is dead love live the king.

it won't be long. ageing rockers are,
above all, pro-
fessionals.

2.

                       [learn to overcome
                                  your addictions.

        if you still have your doubts,
                killing someone, even in self-defence,

is not a solution. what do *you* want??

        let's just hope they don't
hear about this in Memphis.

SHADOWY TECHNICIANS

sh(e)

        proven, has

taken   (above, beyond)
  ]the principle

             i(ssue)

    car (n.) leaps out and
                side
                [swipes

  [and] you don't have a *leg*

to *s(t)and* on

NEW OTTAWA POETS   Ian Whistle

four breakfast poems

one
]salt, pepper, ketchup

　[a woman hits a bus,
　 the one I was riding
(the bus, not the woman)
　curve of sidewalk working
against her not for

]although
　fortunate for the weight of transport
　　a car would've hurt like a
　　bastard

two
]brown toast

　[that poet in a postscript, writing
　　beautiful, beautiful
lines overlapping in a medium

　　(well done!)
meals stealing phrases from menus and signs
(figures from speech
　　pontificating
　　over
　　poached eggs, (he) says

you always sounded better through me

three
]two eggs, scrambled

　　[turning slightly
　　Judith's gossamer wings

SHADOWY TECHNICIANS

and steel rail, indicate

the woman next, during
tea and bagel
screams

and leaves, slamming
doors (mumbling)

   (calmly)   — the waitress
]at the table already a damp cloth

four
]coffee, two sugars

  (girl goes by the _____)

pay the bill
pay the bill, quickly
pay the bill
      bill, quickly
         quickly

NEW OTTAWA POETS Ian Whistle

dis-

    lodged. midriff, onthebus,
no bra. stickers, from the waist up.
Canada is a faraway place. no time
for modesty. honestly, she drops by

with vernacular.] we pay the hotel bill
    leave in a rented car
 ,our lives in the hands again.
someone else stabbed in our room

a day later.

take

    al (on) anon
   ]turid, sparse

making, only
turn turn turn
 /slowburn, misty

    smoke , ahhhh
sliding up, oh

    glom-m-m-

NEW OTTAWA POETS

NEW OTTAWA POETS

Acknowledgements

This page constitutes a continuation of the copyright notice on page 2.

Stephanie Bolster's poems herein have previously appeared in *Canadian Literature*, *Licking Honey Off a Thorn: An Anthology of Poems from the Ontario Division of the League of Canadian Poets*, *(W)rites of Spring, 1998* (1998, Catchfire Press), *Poetry Canada Review*, *Missing Jacket*, *Qwerty*, *Prairie Schooner*, *Descant* & an above/ground press **poem** broadsheet. **Richard Carter**'s poems appeared in *Yield* & an above/ground press **poem** broadsheet. **Laurie Fuhr** previously published in the chapbook *accident* (1999, above/ground press), *graffito* & an above/ground press **poem** broadsheet. Some of **Robin Hannah**'s poems are from *gift of screws* (1997, Broken Jaw Press). **Jim Larwill**'s poems appeared in *Carleton Arts Review*, *I Whisper Love* (Canadian Shield), *SPEAK!: Six Omnigothic Neofuturists* (1997, Broken Jaw Press), *Whiplash 2 Reader* (1997, above/ground press) & *Yield*. **Clare Latremouille** poems' previously appeared in *paperplates*, *graffito*, *the poetry poster* (+ *electronic graffito*), *STANZAS*, *Written in the Skin* (1998, Insomniac Press), *Missing Jacket*, various above/ground press **poem** broadsheets & in the chapbook *I will write a poem for you. Now:* (1995, above/ground press). **Karen Massey**'s poems have appeared in *Bywords*, *Missing Jacket*, *The Windhorse Reader: Best Poems of 1993* (1994, Samurai Press), *Strong Winds* (1997, Broken Jaw Press) & the chapbook *Bullet* (1999, above/ground press). **rob mclennan**'s poems have previously appeared in *The Centretown Buzz*, *Libel!*, *a little something #3* (1999, Broken Jaw Press), *Queen Street Quarterly*, OC Transpo's *transpoetry*, a broadsheet by Ink Link, the chapbook *bagne* (1999, House Press) & various above/ground press **poem** broadsheets. **Ian Whistle**'s work has previously appeared in *The Backwater Review*, *Missing Jacket*, *Written in the Skin* (1998, Insomniac Press) & an above/ground press **poem** broadsheet.

About the Cover and Artist

"This is painterly work that thinks about the object and the viewer's relation to it. In *365 small paintings of chandeliers* Mortson defies any preconceptions about painting as being any kind of fixed thing and challenges the historic treatment and presentation of works in this medium. Mortson's installation is a serial work, an example of painting functioning as a kind of strategic thinking. As in the works of such artists as Cliff Eyland and Gerard Collins, the use of serial imagery in Mortson's installation serves to undercut any propensity to treat each work as discrete. She has treated painting as an installation process, creating on, environment with one, multi-unit, work. In doing so she followed a rules-based process, with pre-determined content, size and quantity. In this work, the action of painting is as important as the content of the work, if not more so. Mortson's work points beyond itself because she questions the medium in the very act of using it. *365 small paintings of chandeliers* is a thoughtful interrogation of a resilient medium, and, not incidentally, a beautiful, singular, painting."
— Ray Cronin, Gallery Connexion, Fredericton, NB

Andrea Morton, the artist, currently lives in Sackville, New Brunswick. Since her studies at the Etobicoke School of the Arts and at Queen's University in Kingston, Andrea has exhibited her work across Canada including at Artcite, Windsor Printmakers' Forum and Common Ground Art Gallery in Windsor ON, Gallery Connexion in Fredericton, Owens Art Gallery in Sackville NB, Thunder Bay Art Gallery, Maintoba Printmakers, Agnes Etherington Art Centre in Kingston ON.

A Selection of Our Titles in Print

A Lad from Brantford (David Adams Richards) essays	0-921411-25-1	11.95
All the Other Phil Thompsons Are Dead (Phil Thompson) poetry	1-896647-05-7	12.95
A View from the Bucket: A Grand Lake and McNabs Island Memoir (Jean Redekopp) memoir, history	0-921411-52-9	14.95
Best in Life: A Guide to Managing Your Relationships ... (Ted Mouradian) self-development, business	0-921411-55-3	18.69
CHSR Poetry Slam (Andrew Titus, ed) poetry	1-896647-06-5	10.95
Combustible Light (Matt Santateresa) poetry	0-921411-97-9	12.95
Cover Makes a Set (Joe Blades) poetry	0-919957-60-9	8.95
Crossroads Cant (Mary Elizabeth Grace, Mark Seabrook, Shafiq, Ann Shin. Joe Blades, editor) poetry	0-921411-48-0	13.95
Dark Seasons (Georg Trakl; Robin Skelton, trans.) poetry	0-921411-22-7	10.95
Dividing the Fire (Robert B. Richards) poetry	1-896647-15-4	4.95
Elemental Mind (K.V. Skene) poetry	1-896647-16-2	10.95
for a cappuccino on Bloor (kath macLean) poetry	0-921411-74-X	13.95
Gift of Screws (Robin Hannah) poetry	0-921411-56-1	12.95
Heart-Beat of Healing (Denise DeMoura)	1-896647-27-8	4.95
Heaven of Small Moments (Allan Cooper) poetry	0-921411-79-0	12.95
Herbarium of Souls (Vladimir Tasic) short fiction	0-921411-72-3	14.95
I Hope It Don't Rain Tonight (Phillip Igloliorti) poetry	0-921411-57-X	11.95
Like Minds (Shannon Friesen) short fiction	0-921411-81-2	14.95
Manitoba highway map (rob mclennan) poetry	0-921411-89-8	13.95
Memories of Sandy Point, St. George's Bay, Newfoundland (Phyllis Pieroway) memoir, history	0-921411-33-2	14.95
New Power (Christine Lowther) poetry	0-921411-94-4	11.95
Notes on drowning (rob mclennan) poetry	0-921411-75-8	13.95
Open 24 Hours (Anne Burke, D.C. Reid, Brenda Niskala Joe Blades, rob mclennan) poetry	0-921411-64-2	13.95
Railway Station (karl wendt) poetry	0-921411-82-0	11.95
Reader be Thou Also ready (Robert James) novel	1-896647-26-X	18.69
Rum River (Raymond Fraser) short fiction	0-921411-61-8	16.95
Seeing the World with One Eye (Edward Gates) poetry	0-921411-69-3	12.95
Shadowy:Technicians: New Ottawa Poets (rob mclennan, ed.)	0-921411-71-5	15.95
Song of the Vulgar Starling (Eric Miller) poetry	0-921411-93-6	14.95
Speaking Through Jagged Rock (Connie Fife) poetry	0-921411-99-5	12.95
Tales for an Urban Sky (Alice Major) poetry	1-896647-11-1	13.95
The Longest Winter (Julie Doiron, Ian Roy) photos & fiction	0-921411-95-2	18.69
Túnel de proa verde / Tunnel of the Green Prow (Nela Rio; Hugh Hazelton, translator) poetry	0-921411-80-4	13.95
Unfolding Fern (Robert B. Richards) poetry	0-921411-98-7	3.00
Wharves and Breakwaters of Yarmouth County, Nova Scotia (Sarah Petite) art/nonfiction	1-896647-13-8	17.95
What Morning Illuminates (Suzanne Hancock) poetry	1-896647-18-9	4.95
What Was Always Hers (Uma Parameswaran) fiction	1-896647-12-X	17.95

www.brokenjaw.com hosts our current products catalogue as well as our submissions guidelines, manuscript award competitions, booktrade sales representation, order fulfilment and sales information including secure eComm. Directly from us, all individual orders must be prepaid. All Canadian orders must add 7% GST/HST (Canada Customs and Revenue Agency GST/HST Number 12489 7943 RT0001). BROKEN JAW PRESS, Box 596 Stn A, Fredericton NB E3B 5A6, Canada.